AMAZON

AMAZON

A YOUNG READER'S LOOK AT THE LAST FRONTIER

BY PETER LOURIE
PHOTOGRAPHS BY MARCOS SANTILLI

BOYDS MILLS PRESS

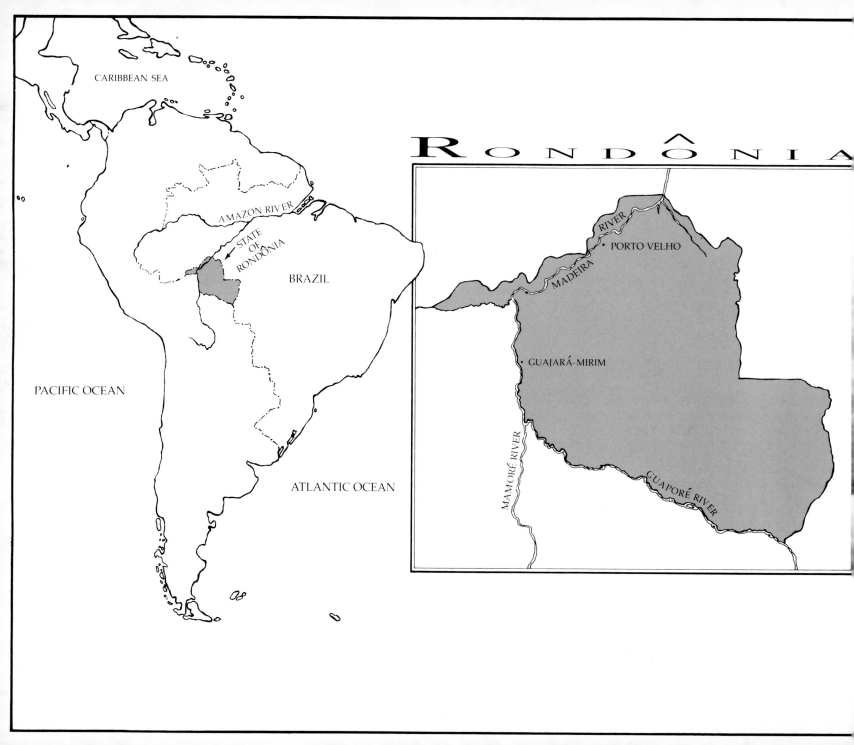

CONTENTS

1
THE RIVER AND RUBBER

We heard the Amazon was vanishing. Colonists were invading the planet's greatest tropical rain forest, felling and burning the trees to grow crops and raise cattle. So two Brazilian friends and I set out for Rondônia, the heart of the Amazon basin, to document what was happening there. We wanted to see what was left of the ancient South American jungle before it disappeared. Our journey began on the Guaporé, a quiet river off the main branch of the Amazon, the great river that flows 3,900 miles from the snow-capped Andes Mountains eastward to the Atlantic.

7

We glided slowly upstream along the banks—Bolivia on the right and Brazil on the left. Tall dark green trees and thick bushes sloped down to the surface of the water. The air was heavy as if after a rain, and the forest had the sharp odor of rotting earth and tropical flowers. Cicadas whined throughout the long, hot, muggy day. The sun was a hazy yellow ball high in the sky.

One sign that civilization had not yet arrived was the presence of the Amazon porpoise. In the evening, after the river calmed, and after we'd pulled up to the shore, silver arcs broke the brown water. Pinkish red bodies rolled on the surface, and through whalelike spouts they exhaled a loud rush of air, then dove out of sight. Some of the Indians who have lived in these jungles for thousands of years refuse to hunt the porpoise because they consider them humanlike, magical creatures. It is said that they will swim up to people who are drowning and help them to shore. Farther downriver, where the settlers have already formed towns and cut the jungle, the porpoise have been hunted so much that few are left. This is sad. They are very beautiful.

While my friend Marlui recorded the sounds of the porpoise, her husband Marcos took a photograph, perhaps the only one of its kind, that shows the Amazon porpoise working together for their meal of tiny fish.

We journeyed to a small village along the Bolivian side of the river where the settlers had cleared the jungle and built their huts on the tall bank. Above us excited children's voices broke the drowsy spell of humidity. We found a one-room schoolhouse with walls made of bark. It stood in a grove of beautiful orange and lemon trees. Children came from miles up and down the river to attend school here.

Many of the Amazon settlers come from rural areas in the South and Southeast of Brazil, where they were landless peasants or sharecroppers. Like pioneers who settled the American West, these children and their families live rugged lives. In this village, for instance, there was no running water or refrigeration, no ice, and no electricity.

Far up the Guaporé we met a rubber tapper named Paulo. A rubber tapper collects latex from a rubber tree just as a farmer taps a maple tree for its sap.

Paulo took us into the forest late at night. He followed a trail he knew by heart, and we watched as he cut a large V in the bark of each tree. Then he placed a little cup at the base of the V to catch the latex. Later he would return to collect the white latex in the cup. It was hard to imagine rubber being harvested in the form of a liquid. Paulo whistled in the darkness. He smoked a hand-rolled cigarette to keep away the bugs. He wore a special metal helmet that focused a flaming wick lamp on the tree. Paulo told us that he worked at night because the jungle is cooler then. But there are dangers in the jungle after dark. Snakes and jaguars, for instance.

The night we went into the jungle to photograph Paulo cutting trees was eerie. The sounds of the insects and frogs came, it seemed, from nowhere and yet from all places, too. I was afraid of putting my hand on a branch that might turn out to be a snake.

Up close to the tree, we could hear the drip drip drip as the beautiful white milk of the latex ran down the grooves into the little cup. When I put my finger into the latex, it was cold and sticky, but runny like real milk. It looked so good I wanted to drink it. But the smell of latex was pungent and cheesy, like wet tires. Later, when we returned for the afternoon harvesting, the latex had already hardened into an elastic, dark gluey matter.

When we got back, Paulo began heating and smoking the latex until he could roll it into a big bundle around a stick. These hardened bundles made it easier for Paulo to transport the rubber to market.

Rubber tappers like Paulo live in harmony with the jungle. Today the rubber tappers and the Indians represent the older, more traditional life in the jungle. Because of the threat of deforestation, the rubber tappers and the Indians have joined forces to defend the rain forest. But only a hundred miles away from Paulo's rubber trees, bulldozers were clearing the jungle for a road that would bring cars and colonists by the thousands.

2
THE DEVIL'S RAILROAD

Along the road we found the mysterious remains of the Devil's Railroad. Coming upon old railroad cars and steam engines overgrown by jungle was like discovering ancient ruins.

During the great rubber boom, the Devil's Railroad had been built from Porto Velho to Guajará-Mirim on the Bolivian border to reach an important rubber-producing part of the Amazon. It took forty years to finish only 227 miles of track. Many people died from tropical diseases like malaria, beri-beri, and dysentery. Hundreds of railroad workers died in clashes with Indians, and the Indians were shot and even electrocuted when they tried to steal the track, making the construction of this railroad one of the most difficult in the world.

15

Begun in 1872, the track wasn't completed until 1912. To build a railroad so far from civilization was as great an engineering challenge as building the Panama Canal. British and American construction companies tried and failed repeatedly. The rails were flooded in the rainy season. The equipment rusted in the jungle humidity. And most of all, sickness made the men too weak to work.

One group of unhappy workers tried to escape into the jungle and were never heard from again. There was a major revolt against the cruel labor conditions. Rebels were thrown into outdoor jails made of steel tracks, where at night they would go crazy from the mosquitoes. We photographed one of these jails—the last in existence.

After only a few miles of track were put down, one-third of the labor force was either dead or in the hospital. Finally, in 1907, thirty-five years after the railroad was started, an American captain of industry named Percival Farquhar built a huge construction camp. Farquhar was smart. He realized that the railroad could not be completed unless he won the war against the anopheles mosquito, which carries malaria, by far the most devastating disease in the area. He sprayed the swamps with pesticides. He passed out malaria medicine to his workers. And in the next five years, Farquhar's company completed the track from Porto Velho to Guajará-Mirim. The train's bell clanged through the jungle like a miracle. But what a sacrifice it had been to build! Thousands of people had died. Some say that every railroad tie on the tracks represents a worker who lost his life. This may be an exaggeration, but it illustrates the way people felt about the project. And that's one reason they call it the Devil's Railroad.

Then another terrible event happened. The year that the Devil's Railroad was completed, the rubber boom in Brazil crashed. In 1912 the British managed to establish organized rubber plantations in the Far East, where rubber could be grown and harvested much more efficiently than in the jungle. It became too expensive to transport Rondônian rubber to Europe and the United States. So the Devil's Railroad languished.

From 1912 to 1972 the train ran only a few times a week. Then in 1972 the Brazilian government closed the railroad in favor of a new road. Thick vegetation grew over the bridges. The track decayed. The engines began to rust in the jungle. Marcos photographed some local boys climbing on the old steam engines.

A few years before we arrived, the citizens of Porto Velho wanted to restore the old track and get the train running again. They felt it was a large part of their heritage, and they wanted to make a living museum out of the train. After years of neglect, twenty of the 227 miles of track had been restored.

We were fortunate to make a trip on that newly restored line. An old locomotive took us up the track. The whistle screamed in the trees, and the engine clanged, ready for departure. White steam hissed from the pistons around the wheels, and billows of smoke poured out of the stack as we rolled into motion.

We sat on top of the coal car, which was fixed with wood for the firebox. Two men shoved the wood into the flaming boiler. The jungle morning smelled of metal parts and smoke and steam. We felt like pioneers on a maiden run. But we would have to travel backwards up the track because the engine had no place to turn around at the end of the line. In a half hour we reached the jungle where the track had not been cleared yet. Our engine slowed, and the train came to a creaky, hissing stop. It was exciting to ride the old train, but the adventure was over too soon. The whistle screamed again like a salute from another era, and the trainmen got ready for the run back to Porto Velho.

3
GOLD

From the tracks we walked down to the wide Madeira River, the largest tributary of the Amazon. The river was named Madeira, which means "wood" in Portuguese, because of all the trees that get washed down from the jungles. We had heard about a gold mining camp downriver, and we wanted to spend a few days there to see how the gold miners lived and worked.

Brazil is one of the world's biggest producers of gold, and much of the gold is mined in such camps. During the dry season in Rondônia as many as fifteen thousand miners had come to find their fortune here, and by 1990 that number had increased to sixty thousand.

There are three main ways to mine for gold in the Amazon. One is to dig and sift the dirt for gold dust. Another is to pan for gold in the water along the river shore. But by far the most effective mining technique is to dive off rafts in the middle of the river and to vacuum the gold from the riverbed.

The men panning for gold stand in the water with two kinds of pans. The quality of the deposit, how much gold the sand contains, is first tested in a smaller pan. When the sand promises enough gold, the miner changes to a larger, flatter pan. He lets a little water into the pan and swirls the sand and water. Then he lets a little water out. The lighter particles of dirt are carried out over the edge of the pan. The heavier gold flakes remain at the bottom. This process takes time and experience. After the gold is mostly separated, it gleams in the pan like bits of sunlight. Then the miner adds silvery liquid mercury. Unlike the finer sand, the fine gold flecks adhere to the mercury. Later he heats this mixture until it bonds into a conglomerate of gold. Then he sells his gold in this form to the gold dealers. (In recent years, the amount of mercury that gets into the river systems has become a real hazard to the fish and the plants.)

In the distance we could see a fleet of wooden rafts with bright blue and yellow plastic awnings. They seemed like a mirage in a desert—but on a river! As we approached we heard the purr of their pumps and compressors. These motors would run all day and night for months without stopping. Each raft ran two hoses into the water, one sending air down to the diver himself, and the other sucking the sand and gravel off the riverbed, which contained some of the richest gold deposits in the Amazon basin.

One diver wore the old-fashioned, deep-sea bell helmet. Most wore the more common masks that fit over the eyes and nose. With one hand, the divers held a hose to their mouths so they could breathe; in the other hand they gripped the wider hose that sucked the muck off the bottom of the dark river. This sandy gravel was then pumped up to the raft where it was filtered and screened through a series of wooden trays.

On the Madeira, each raft could dredge up as much as fifty grams of gold in a seven-hour period, or thirty-five pounds a month. In four months, a raft could bring in as much as 150 pounds of gold.

But when gold miners reach the cities after a season in camp, many spend their money fast, and before long they are poor again. Then they return the next year for more gold.

Marcos spoke to the men in Portuguese, the language of Brazil, but many of them were reluctant to talk. Maybe they thought we might steal their gold. Most miners hide their gold in the jungle, and carry guns to protect their claims, their stashes, and themselves. These mining camps could be dangerous places. Everyone on the Madeira seemed very watchful of others.

We felt lucky to have visited the gold miners of Rondônia and to have witnessed the wild life they lead. But we still needed to drive down the dirt highway to the frontier, where the colonists were burning the jungle.

4
THE ROAD AND THE FIRE

We traveled in my friends' Jeep along what is known simply as the BR-364, a dirt road that had been cut like a long scar through the middle of Rondônia. The road was in terrible condition with ruts and potholes the size of elephants.

It is amazing how fast the rain forest can turn to dust when the thick, green jungle is cut and burned. Along the road going south from the capital, the colonists had cleared thousands and thousands of acres for farms and pastures. The area was so dry that the violet dust rose into the air and covered absolutely everything. Our camera equipment, our hair, and our skin were layered with the fine Rondônian dust. It clogged our nostrils and made it hard to breathe.

The state of Rondônia, an area about the size of Wyoming, or twice the size of England, was entirely jungle a few decades ago. But now much of it has been turned into towns and a network of roads. Colonists have been flooding into the state since the 1970s, when the government of Brazil began encouraging people to move here. Rondônia is just one of the Amazon states colonized by hundreds of thousands of people looking for a better life. Families arrive in the Amazon from all parts of Brazil. They come from regions of drought and famine, they come from overcrowded cities, and they hope to find Paradise here in the jungle. Sometimes four or five families will come in one run-down old truck, which is like the covered wagon of the American West. Brazilians call these trucks "Macaws' Perches" because they have very narrow, hard wooden seats. And they carry all the colonists' belongings, which are as colorful as tropical birds: all their chickens, pigs, furniture, pets, and clothes—everything.

Although the colonists are seeking a good life, they often find it very hard in Amazonia. They are threatened by rampant diseases like malaria. And the land is difficult to farm. When settlers first arrive, they cut and burn the jungle so they can begin to grow crops like coffee and cacao. Unfortunately, after only a few years these kinds of crops deplete the delicate jungle soil, and soon the land grows so dry it turns to a near desert. And the colonists move on.

The fastest way to get rid of the jungle is to cut and burn it during the dry months of August and September. We traveled during this dry season and saw so many fires burning along the roads that the sky had turned to a blue haze.

This colonization of the Amazon is much like what happened in the American West in the 1800s. When the West was settled, railroads were built, buffalo were killed, and the prairies were cultivated. But what took eighty years to accomplish in the United States will take far fewer years in the Amazon with bulldozers and other modern machinery. The Amazon basin, with its network of hundreds and hundreds of rivers, was inaccessible for ages. This huge area (the basin is a little smaller than the continental United States) supplies a fifth of the earth's fresh water and includes one third of its tropical rain forest. But the wilderness is vanishing quickly. Perhaps colonization is necessary in a modern world, and Brazil is following in the footsteps of many other nations. But the planet will lose these precious few remaining rain forests with the coming of civilization.

Today many scientists believe that loss of the jungle means we will lose fauna and flora that have not yet been studied. The Amazon harbors many thousand species of plants and many million animal and insect species, an estimated one-fifth of all the world's bird species, and perhaps eight times as many kinds of fish as in the Mississippi River and its tributaries. Some scientists are also worried about the carbon dioxide produced from all the fires burning in the Amazon. They fear this will add to the layer of carbon dioxide and other gases from burning fossil fuels. Although burning the rain forests contributes much less than automobile emissions, the accumulated carbon forms a layer of gas, scientists believe, that prevents too little of the warmth created from the sun's rays from escaping back into space. This heat then builds up and creates what is known as the Greenhouse Effect, which some scientists fear might lead to excessive global warming.

We followed the road farther south through more and more burning jungle. As we approached the fires, the air got hotter and hotter until it was too hot to take pictures. We wanted to get back to the cool river. We'd seen too much burning and too many people destroying ancient jungle. So we decided to visit an Indian tribe in a part of Rondônia still untouched by the colonists.

5
INDIANS

My friends and I rented a small boat with only a canvas tarp as a roof. We went for miles on a small tributary of the Mamoré River, which was very narrow in places. Clusters of tangled palm trees hung over the banks. It seemed as if no one had ever been up this river before. There were no houses here, no television, no roads, and no colonists—at least not yet. We could tell the rainy season was coming. Each day it rained a little more. Huge rain clouds formed and dissolved over the great forest. After a few days' travel, we reached the Indian outpost. Dusk was falling quickly, and the frogs on shore began to croak.

These Indians were far enough away from civilization that they could live much like they had for centuries. But even here certain changes had come. The children were not learning the old customs. They could not sing the old tribal songs. The elders found this sad. Marlui, who had brought her guitar, sang a song of her own. The children sat around her and sang songs that the missionaries had taught them.

The high point of our visit was the fishing trip. More than thirty of us walked through a flurry of butterflies by the thousands until we came to a small river in a clearing. When we reached a place where the river formed a natural pool, the boys went into the jungle to look for lianas from a timbó tree. They dragged the long, snakelike lianas back to the river and cut them into pieces a few feet long. They waded into the water and beat the wood together hard and fast. From the splintering fibers, a natural poison spread out into the pool.

In about an hour, when the chemical had taken effect, the fish began to float to the surface. Most of them were stunned but not yet dead. With bare hands the boys and girls scooped up the fish and tossed them onto the beach. Other children laughed and gathered the fish in piles. Some used bows and arrows to spear the fish that had not yet floated to the surface.

We were witnesses to the old Indian life, the life that had been going on here for thousands of years. But having seen the road and the fires of the burning jungle not far away, we knew this life and the peace of the jungle would be shattered forever. There would be the sound of chain saws in the forest and the sound of the roaring jungle in flames. Perhaps there would be no more plants that made the chemical needed to stun the fish. And this kind of simple fishing trip might soon disappear.

The next day we got back into our boat. The Indians waved good-bye. The sky was clearing. The strong winds from the Andes that preceded the heavy rains were wiping away the smoke and dust from the roads in the South. The dry season was ending and the mud season was on its way.

We had seen the untouched Amazon and the invasion of urban civilization. We had seen tribal life and the isolated life of the rubber tapper. We had seen the Devil's Railroad and the camp of the hard-living gold miners. Most striking perhaps was our impression of the burning rain forest. Those fires seemed to have burned images of flame and smoke into our hearts.

Now as we left the tribal outpost and headed back the way we had come, we glided downriver with the soft, slow, ancient current. There was something moving in the river—something playful and magic breaking the water's calm. There they were! Five porpoises rose and dove and swam around our boat as if to say good-bye forever.

FUNDING FOR THE PHOTOGRAPHIC PROJECT WAS PROVIDED BY
THE JOHN SIMON GUGGENHEIM MEMORIAL FOUNDATION.—M.S.

FOR SUZANNA ADELE LOURIE—P.L.

Published by Caroline House
Boyds Mills Press, Inc.
A Highlights Company
815 Church Street
Honesdale, Pennsylvania 18431
First Boyds Mills Press paperback edition 1998
Printed in Hong Kong
Book designed by Abby Kagan

Publisher Cataloging-in-Publication Data

Lourie, Peter.
  Amazon: A Young Reader's Look at the Last Frontier/by Peter Lourie; photographs by Marcos
Santilli.
  48p.:col. ill.; cm
Summary: A first-hand account of a journey through the Brazilian state of Rondonia, the very
heart of the Amazon. Highlights the rubber and gold exploration, the Devil's Railroad and
Indians, and finally, the burning of the jungle.
Hardcover ISBN 1-878093-00-2 Paperback ISBN 1-56397-712-5
1. Brazil—Description and travel—Juvenile Literature. 2. Amazon River—Juvenile Literature.
[1. Brazil—Description and travel. 2. Amazon River.] I. Santilli, Marcos, ill. II. Title.
918.1/063-dc20   1991
LC 90-85720

Hardcover 10 9 8 7 6 5 4 3 2 1
Paperback 10 9 8 7 6 5 4 3 2 1